ONE Chick TO Another

GIBBS SMITH
TO ENRICH AND INSPIRE HUMANKIND

I feel pretty,
oh so pretty!

A true friend
is one who thinks
you're a good egg
—even if
you're half cracked.

A wise old rooster once said, "You keep flappin' your gums like that and you'll get your tongue sun burnt."

Shouldn't we be wearing helmets?

She's finally
flown the coop!

It's easier to count your chickens before they've hatched.

She was often thought of as a chicken outstanding in her field.

It's best not
to keep all of your
chicks
in one basket.

Wow!
I think you
coughed
a little too hard
this time.

I just can't
get clucking
without my morning
cup o' joe.

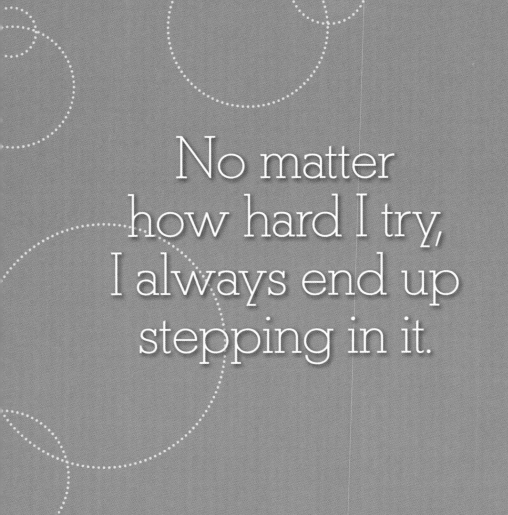

No matter
how hard I try,
I always end up
stepping in it.

Attaching feathers to your fanny doesn't make you a chicken.

Mildred
was feeling a little
pecked on
by the other hens.

Well, butter my butt and call me a biscuit!

That was one
crazy rooster!

Chicks—
delighting in
our similarities,
celebrating
our differences.

Do these
feathers make my butt
look big?

Life isn't all
it's cracked
up to be.

Say hello to
my little friend.

Hangin'
with my peeps.

The rooster
may rule the roost,
but the hen
rules the rooster.

Nobody
said it would be easy.

I heard the exotic look was in this year.

I've been
on a diet for
two weeks now,
and the only thing
I've lost is
fourteen days.

What happens
in the coop
stays in the coop.

Her drumsticks went all the way up to her thighs.

Having a
bad feather day.

I'm sooo out of here!

Well, that just flaps my wattle!

Momma always said
that life is like
a box of chicklets.

Beauty—
it's a burden
that I must
carry.

Dance as though
no one is watching,
and cluck as if
no one can hear.

If momma
ain't happy,
ain't nobody
happy.

You're the yin
to my yang.

Let me guess, dearie—you're lookin' for a husband?

Bring it on chickie!

I put the "fab"
in fabulous.

First Edition
23 22 21 20   10 9 8 7 6

Published by
Gibbs Smith
P.O. Box 667
Layton, Utah 84041

1.800.835.4993 orders
www.gibbs-smith.com

Edited by the Gibbs Smith Barn staff
Designed by Debra McQuiston
Printed and bound in China

Gibbs Smith books are printed on either
recycled, 100% post-consumer waste, FSC-
certified papers or on paper produced from
sustainable PEFC-certified forest/controlled
wood source. Learn more at www.pefc.org.

ISBN 978-1-4236-1836-2

Photo Credits

Photos from Shutterstock, © 2011 as follows:

Pakhnyushcha, back cover
Antonioa Jorge Nunes,
    front cover
Africa Studio, 1
Cynoclub, 3
Ariusz Nawrocki, 4
Richard Peterson, 7
Karen Roach, 8
Marcel Jancovic, 11
Val R, 12
Bas Meelker, 15
Klimona, 16
Thomas Sereda, 23

Vishnevskly Vasily, 19, 48
Shmel, 20
Thomas Sereda, 23
Sebastian Duda, 24, 55
Lucertolone, 27
Anna Sedneva, 28, 64
Ivonne Wierink, 31
Perrush, 32
Poznukhov Yurly, 35
Gelpi, 36
Eric Isselé, 39, 52, 56, 60,
    71, 79
Vasyl Helevachuk, 40, 47

VT750, 43
Goran Kuzmanovski, 44
Kemeo, 51
Jeremy Richards, 59
Cameilia, 63
Jasiek03, 67
MilousSK, 68
Mashe, 72
Dmitriy Shironosov, 75
Irin-k, 76